For my mum, who looks after
my park when I am away
A

For my amma Birgitta, who
always waited by the window
for me. I miss you and carry
you always in my heart.
BS

• First US edition 2021 • First published by Walker Books (UK) 2020 • Library of Congress Catalog Card Number pending • ISBN 978-1-5362-1275-4 • This book was typeset in Architype Regular. The illustrations were done in pencil and colored digitally.
Candlewick Press, 99 Dover Street, Somerville, Massachusetts 02144 • www.candlewick.com
Printed in Heshan, Guangdong, China • 21 22 23 24 25 26 LEO 10 9 8 7 6 5 4 3 2 1

HUGO

Atinuke

illustrated by Birgitta Sif

CANDLEWICK PRESS

My name is Hugo.
I am a park warden.
I look after the park,
and I look after the people
who live around it.
It is my job.

In the spring,
I encourage Monsieur
Petit to take his walk.

I keep Madame
Grande company
as she sits in the sun.

I discuss the news with Monsieur Occupé.

In the summer,
I do my best to clean up . . .

after Minou

and Chérie and Puce

and all their friends and relations.

In the autumn, I help to entertain Bébé
and Coquine so their mothers can rest.

And in the winter,
I visit everybody.
I remind them that
spring will be here before long.

But there is one window
where the curtains are never open.
I still visit. I knock politely.
I see somebody hide whenever
they hear a sound.

Then one day
I see Somebody!

I do my
spring-is-coming
dance and Somebody
smiles a little smile.

Now every day Somebody is waiting.
Waiting to hear me knock.
Waiting to see me dance.

Until the day that I am late . . .

and Somebody opens the window!
Somebody leans out to look for me!

I am so happy
I do a showing-off
dance on the bench.

I do not see the dog . . .

until it is too late!

Somebody cries,

"Non!"

When I wake up, my wing hurts.
I do not want to hop.
I know I cannot fly.

Somebody brings
me water.

Somebody brings
me crumbs.

Somebody strokes
my wing.

Then one day
I can hop, hop, hop!
Somebody laughs and
claps for me!

I hop to the window.
I knock politely.
Somebody shakes
her head.

I knock again.
And again.

Somebody looks so sad.
She wants me to stay
here with her.

But I knock and knock and knock
until Somebody opens the window for me.
She does not want me to be sad,
so she has to let me go.

I hop onto the windowsill
and flutter to the ground.

I hop and hop toward the bench.
It takes a long, long time.

I am so tired I rest my beak
on the ground.

Monsieur Petit, Madame Grande,
Monsieur Occupé, Minou,
Chérie, Puce, Bébé, and Coquine
all come to their windows and cheer
and cheer and cheer me on!

I flutter to the park bench
to do my little dance.

"Non!" Somebody cries.

But it is only Monsieur Petit's dog.
He is my old friend.

But who is this running to save me?

Does she want to play?

I cock my head.
Somebody smiles!

Up and down and up and down

and up and down we go . . .

until Somebody is laughing.

And all the children run out
to play with her.

"Aimée!"
her mother calls.

And all the children join in.
"Aimée! Aimée! Aimée!"

My name is Hugo.

I am a park warden.
I look after the park,
and I look after the people
who live here.
It is my job.

I love my job!